Kafka
and the
Doll

Kafka
and the
Doll

LARISSA THEULE   REBECCA GREEN

VIKING

One autumn day, the writer Franz Kafka and Dora Diamant strolled through a park in Berlin. Kafka held a basket filled with potatoes and a jar of milk. His hat was set at an angle and he walked deep in thought about two things: a story he was struggling to finish, and lunch.

He kicked through leaves, pulling at the collar of
his shirt and pausing to cough into his handkerchief.

Nearby, a girl stood crying.

Kafka said, "Why the tears?"

"My doll is lost," said the girl.

"I see," said Kafka. "What is her name?"

"Soupsy."

"And you are?"

"Irma."

Kafka nodded.
"I thought as much.
Your Soupsy is not lost
but traveling, as dolls
like to do.
She wrote
you a letter."

Irma frowned.
"Where is the
letter?"

"At home in the pocket of my overcoat," said Kafka. "I'm a volunteer postman, you see. I will bring you the letter tomorrow. Just now I'm off to lunch."

Irma's frown deepened.

Kafka said, "Potatoes, if you must know."

The following day, Irma waited.
Kafka delivered the letter.

October 23, 1923

Darling Irma, forgive me for not saying goodbye. The bicycle was passing, the basket lay empty, and I did not think—I simply jumped in. I have always been one for adventure, as you know. Please do not be cross. I am on a train on my way to go hiking. The air here smells like those flowers your mother likes so well, I never did learn the name.

You are always in my heart,
Soupsy

"Well?" said Kafka.

"She went hiking."

He nodded. "It's a beautiful time of year for hiking. She'll write again, of course. People on adventures like to tell about them."

October 24, 1923

Irma, I hiked to the very top! As I write I am watching the sunrise from above a cloud. The world turns softly purple, which is not my favorite color, but when the world wears it, I think it just fine.

You are always in my heart,
Soupsy

"And?" said Kafka.

"She hiked to the very top."

"Bravo."

October 25, 1923

Hello, I am in Paris! And have eaten
croissants for breakfast, lunch, and dinner.
In fact, I have eaten nothing but what
pleases me since leaving Berlin. How can
I face a carrot stick when I might have
a peppermint stick? What use to me
is a bowl of peas when I might have
crème brûlée?

You are always in my heart,
Soupsy

"I don't understand this drawing," said Irma.

Kafka studied the postcard.

"Obviously, it's the countryside.
Here's the cottage. A goat."

Irma took back the card.

"It's a rabbit, not a goat."

"Yes," said Kafka. "I see it now."

Soupsy traveled to England and had tea with Peter Rabbit.

In Barcelona she joined Gaudí for his daily walk.
He knew wonderful things about architecture.

In Morocco she had warm sfenj and mint tea. She tried to ride a camel but wasn't sure how and dodged neatly away when it spat at her.

She visited the pyramids in Egypt and wondered at the vast
expanse of beauty and sand stretching out below, writing to Irma
that her heart was hurting in a way that told her it was growing.

Soupsy wrote at every stop, but the letters grew short.

November 8, 1923

Dearest Irma, I'm riding down the
Nile on a boat with my new friends.
They're teaching me Arabic and I'm
teaching them German. Salam!

~ S.

"Why so unhappy?" said Kafka.

"All of me is growing," said Irma.

"Mama says I need new shoes."

Kafka studied his own shoes. "These will last."

Leaves blew in little cyclones around their feet.

Kafka pulled out his handkerchief.

"My grandpa had that cough," said Irma. "It never went away."

One day Kafka did not visit the market
and so he did not walk through the park.

Irma waited.

She walked home.

Again she waited.

Again she walked home.

"Where is Herr Kafka?" demanded Irma.

"He has a headache behind his eyes that won't go away," said Dora.
"But never would he neglect his obligations as postman. A letter for you,
from your Soupsy."

"You are," whispered Irma.

"You're pale," said Irma.

Kafka smiled. "You miss nothing."

Hesitantly, Irma held out her hand. A certainty came over her. This letter would be the last.

November 12, 1923

Dearest Irma, I have signed on for an expedition to the desolate ends of Antarctica. The journey will be long and arduous. My job is to break up the ice with a pickax so that the boat can go through. Letter writing, I fear, will be impossible, and so this is goodbye. You are bold and you are brave, and I am proud to have been, for a time, your beloved doll.

Your Soupsy

Irma folded the letter. "She left on an expedition."

"Expeditions are grand affairs from what I understand. Important discoveries to be made, and all that," said Kafka.

"She won't be back," said Irma.

All through the park, barren trees poked fingers into the belly of the gray sky.

"Someday, I will travel,"
said Irma. "I'd like to ride a camel."
"Be on guard for spitting."
"I know about that already."

"And carry a notebook and pen with you wherever you go so that your adventures remain," said Kafka. His shoulders folded in as he coughed.

Irma waited.

Kafka straightened, his smile gentle. "Goodbye now, Irma."
"Goodbye, Herr Kafka."

Their warm breath clung fiercely to the cold air, then blew
softly away, one to play and explore and one, finally, to sleep.

AUTHOR'S NOTE

In the fall of 1923, Franz Kafka lived in Berlin with Dora Diamant, his last and truest love. Despite Kafka's illness and having little money, they shared a contented happiness the writer had been searching for his whole life.

One day while walking through the park, Kafka and Dora met a little girl who was crying because she'd lost her doll. Moved by the girl's grief, Kafka told her the doll was not lost, only traveling. For three weeks he wrote letters to the girl from her doll and through the power of storytelling helped ease the loss of her beloved friend. He devoted as much thought to the letters as to his work.

Many years later Dora relayed these events to Kafka's biographer Marthe Robert. People tried to find the girl and the letters but no one did. The girl remains unidentified and the letters lost. Dora's account is all we have.

Dora said Kafka struggled to know how to end the letter campaign and finally decided to have the doll get married and start a family of her own. Most likely this reflected the girl's understanding of the world and her own place in it, for girls in the 1920s had few options for their futures apart from marriage. But times have changed, and I felt the ending should reflect the wide world of possible futures available to children (and dolls!) today, which is why I sent Soupsy on a scientific expedition to Antarctica. If one day down the road, however, Soupsy chooses to adventure with a partner, I think that would be lovely.

As for Soupsy's letters, her voice is all my own—no one can write like Kafka. My one hope is they succeed in communicating Kafka's intent to heal a child's wounded heart. Rebecca Green's choice to show Kafka giving Irma a journal honors the writer's own commitment to journaling. He often used the medium as a creative outlet when his stories refused to cooperate.

The legend of Kafka and the traveling doll has captivated people's imaginations for decades. We think of Kafka as brooding and grim, like his stories, but the legend reminds us he was also charming and playful. He was a thoughtful person who cared deeply for others.

Kafka died of tuberculosis in June 1924, the spring following his and Dora's brief turn of happiness in Berlin. His writing lives on, and so, I like to think, does his kindness.

BIO

Franz Kafka was born in 1883.

He was the only son of a middle-class Jewish family living in Prague during a time of rapid social and industrial change. He was a sensitive and absorbing child. He had three sisters and was especially fond of the youngest, Ottla, but he never felt close to his father, whom he regarded as harsh and intimidating.

Kafka lived to write. He used everything around him as inspiration for novels and short stories, including family and friends, current events, physical surroundings, and eventually his work as a lawyer for a government insurance agency. He was an avid letter writer and kept a detailed journal. Honest, trusting relationships meant a great deal to him. He was a devoted friend and brother, but he was also constantly in and out of love until he met Dora Diamant.

During his lifetime Kafka published some of what he wrote, to critical acclaim, but his fame didn't come until after he died, thanks to Dora and his good friend Max Brod. Kafka had instructed Dora and Max to burn his papers. Dora did burn some as requested but kept others. Max Brod burned none. Instead he published and championed his friend's work and thereby gave a great gift to the world. Kafka viewed life through a sharp, probing lens and the stories he wrote are disorienting, even nightmarish. His novella *Metamorphosis* is about a young man who slowly turns into a giant insect, much to the disgust and horror of his family.

But even now, nearly a century after his death, the plots and themes of Kafka's stories still resonate. Sometimes life is a bewildering journey.

Franz Kafka in Berlin 1923/1924.
Photo credit: Archive Klaus Wagenbach.

BIBLIOGRAPHY

Adler, Jeremy. *Franz Kafka*. Woodstock and New York: Overlook Press, 2001.

Diamant, Kathi. *Kafka's Last Love*. London: Secker & Warburg, 2003.

Murray, Nicholas. *Kafka: A Biography*. London: Little, Brown, 2004.

Additional reading for kids interested in Franz Kafka:

Roth, Matthue. *My First Kafka: Runaways, Rodents & Giant Bugs*. Long Island City, NY: One Peace Books, Inc., 2013.

For Sonia and Anya Husain
—L.T.

For my friend, Greg Oberle
—R.G.

VIKING
An imprint of Penguin Random House LLC, New York

First published in the United States of America by Viking,
an imprint of Penguin Random House LLC, 2021

LIBRARY OF CONGRESS CATALOGING-IN-PUBLICATION DATA IS AVAILABLE

Manufactured in China

ISBN 9780593116326

1 3 5 7 9 10 8 6 4 2

The art for this book was created digitally.